Quiz.#
21223

P9-CBS-307

ANTHONY BROWNE

WILLY the CHAMP

CANDLEWICK PRESS
CAMBRIDGE, MASSACHUSETTS

First Candlewick Press edition 2002

Library of Congress Cataloging-in-Publication Data

Browne, Anthony.
Willy the Champ / Anthony Browne. —1st Candlewick Press ed.
p.   cm.
Summary: Not very good at sports or fighting, mild-mannered Willy
nevertheless proves he's the champ when the local bully shows up.
ISBN 0-7636-1842-X
[1. Chimpanzees—Fiction. 2. Bullies—Fiction.] I. Title.
PZ7.B81984 Wf 2002
[E]—dc21   2001052496

2 4 6 8 10 9 7 5 3 1

Printed in Hong Kong

This book was typeset in Plantin.
The illustrations were done in watercolor, ink, and colored pencil.

Candlewick Press
2067 Massachusetts Avenue
Cambridge, Massachusetts 02140

visit us at www.candlewick.com

For Ellen

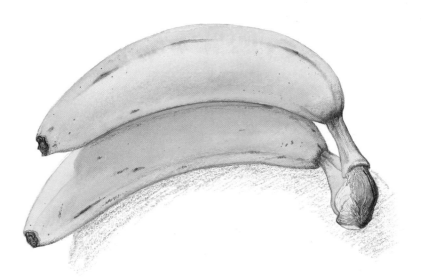

Willy didn't seem to be good at anything.

He liked to read . . .

and listen to music . . .

and walk in the park with his friend, Millie.

Willy wasn't any good at soccer . . .

He did try.

Willy tried bike racing . . .

He really did try.

Sometimes Willy walked to the pool.

Other times he went to the movies with Millie.

But it was always the same. Nearly everyone
laughed at him—no matter what he did.

One day Willy was standing on the corner with the boys when a huge, horrible figure appeared.

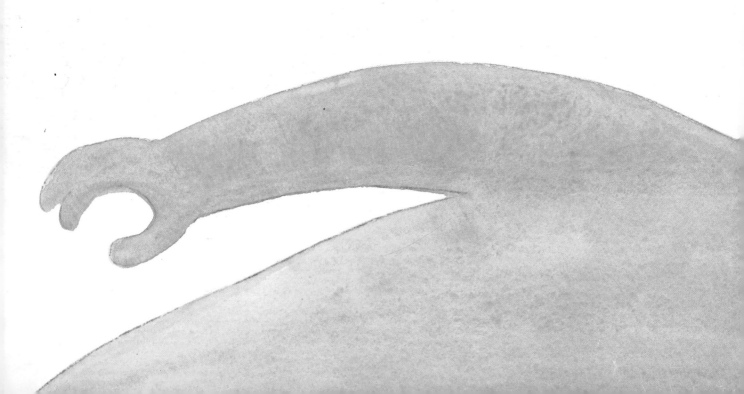

It was Buster Nose.
And he was huge and horrible.

The boys fled.

Buster threw a vicious punch.

Willy ducked . . .

. . . then he stood up!

"Oh, I'm sorry," said Willy, "are you all right?"

Buster went home to his mom.

Willy was the Champ.